Introducing Pop Monsters...

Deep in the heart of the Pacific Northwest there lives a furry band of critters that come in all shapes and sizes. In that wooded glen, among the misty meadows and mossy-bearded trees, they share fun and adventure in a magical place called Wetmore Forest.

STERLING CHILDREN'S BOOKS
New York

An Imprint of Sterling Publishing Co., Inc.
1166 Avenue of the Americas
New York, NY 10036

ISBN 978-1-4549-3603-9

Distributed in Canada by Sterling Publishing Co., Inc.
c/o Canadian Manda Group, 664 Annette Street
Toronto, Ontario M6S 2C8, Canada
Distributed in the United Kingdom by GMC Distribution Services
Castle Place, 166 High Street, Lewes, East Sussex BN7 1XU, England
Distributed in Australia by NewSouth Books, University of New South Wales,
Sydney, NSW 2052, Australia

For information about custom editions, special sales, and premium and corporate purchases, please contact Sterling Special Sales at 800-805-5489 or specialsales@sterlingpublishing.com.

Manufactured in the United States of America
Lot #:
2 4 6 8 10 9 7 5 3 1
07/19

A Tale of Two Tribes

A WETMORE FOREST STORY

By Randy Harvey and Sean Wilkinson
Illustrated by John Skewes

STERLING CHILDREN'S BOOKS
New York

ne day in Wetmore Forest, Snuggletooth and the rest of the gang were getting ready for an important journey.

Every year, it was their job to gather the special herbs and spices that were used to make a delicious feast for the annual Harvest Festival. No one knew the mountains and trails of Wetmore Forest better than Snuggletooth and her friends. Their search often took them to the farthest reaches of the forest, down steep hillsides, and high atop the tallest peaks.

"If we hurry," Snuggletooth told the others, "We should make it to Ayers Rock just in time to see the majestic Blue-Finned Sloops migrate north for the winter!"

Butterhorn, who was calm and very organized, was
in charge of the map. The mountains and forests that
surrounded Wetmore Valley made for very difficult
travel, and it was up to her to make sure they all got
to where they needed to go.

"First stop, Bogwaller Swamp!" Butterhorn announced.

As leader, it was Snuggletooth's job to decide which tasks were best suited to each monster's special talents.

"Okay, guys, here's the plan," said Snuggletooth.

"Picklez will use his superior speed to pick Lily Pods and gather up **Snodgrass shoots** for the Snodgrass Dumplings. Just remember not to step on a Swamp Snapper!"

After gathering mushberries, it's time to get Pitter-pat roots. Chester's brilliant new root-grabber invention should cut the harvest time in half!"

"Then it's on to Black Gulch for some Bitter Blossoms. They only grow in the hardest-to-reach places, but that's no problem for our Bugsy."

"Last stop is Misty Meadows for all the
Sneeze-Wheezies we can carry.
Tumblebee, we're counting on you, buddy!"

With their packs now stuffed full of so many delicious things to eat, the monsters decided it was time to camp for the night. In the morning, they would travel the final leg of their journey to Ayers Rock . . . hopefully just in time to see the migration of the Blue-Finned Sloops!

Later that night, after the monsters had
all fallen fast asleep, two mysterious creatures snuck into
the camp and quietly opened each of the overstuffed packs.

The thieves snatched the
Sneeze-Weezies,

pilfered the
Pitter-pat roots,

and made off with the
mushberries!

The rascals took everything
they could carry . . . and then
scurried off into the night!

The next morning, the Wetmore Monsters awoke and discovered what had happened.

"My backpack is empty!" Bugsy cried. "Someone took my harvest!"

"Tumblebee! Did you eat my mushberries?" Chester demanded. "Stick out your tongue!"

Tumblebee did as he was told, but it was clear that he was innocent.

"Who would do such a thing?" exclaimed Snuggletooth.

"Look here,"
shouted Butterhorn.
"I think I found a clue."

The monsters followed the tracks down a
narrow trail to the riverside. They made their way over
a little stone crossing, and then came to a large rock.
There, they discovered the two culprits.

"Who are you two?" Snuggletooth demanded.
"And why have you stolen our food?"

"I'm Ichenscratch," said the scruffy little monster. "This is Liverwort. We never meant to steal, but we were so hungry!"

"We were on the verge of *starvation*,"
cried Liverwort dramatically.

"You see," Ichenscratch explained, "Where we come from, it's hard to find food. The volcano has choked away the sun with soot and ash, so nothing grows. We have to travel far and wide to find anything to eat."

"That sounds terrible," said Butterhorn. "But it's still not okay to steal. Besides, we would have shared if you just asked."

Suddenly, three other monsters stepped out from the trees. Their leader, who wore a mask, came forward. He looked at Ichenscratch and Liverwort, who looked back at him sheepishly.

"What's going on here?" he asked.

"These two snuck into our camp and stole our food,"
explained Snuggletooth. "Looks like they polished
off most of it, too."

"My name is Grumble," the masked monster said.
"This is Mulch and Tilly. I guess you've already met Ichenscratch
and Liverwort. We have very little food to offer in return for what
was taken. But we do have some fine volcanic chipping stones for
tool making. We could give you these as a trade, if you agree."

"It's a deal," Snuggletooth said, cheerfully.
"We'll restock our harvest on our journey back home.
In the meantime, how about a picnic?"

"I think I have enough mushberries left to make
mushberry tarts," said Butterhorn.

And so the monsters all got to know each other better.
They ate snacks together and told many stories, until
Butterhorn remembered that she and the Wetmore
Monsters needed to leave soon if they were going to
make it to Ayers Rock before they had to return home
for the Harvest Festival.

With the sun setting on the horizon and a perfect view
atop Ayers Rock, friends new and old watched the
Blue-Finned Sloops swim north for the winter.
Sitting together, the far away mountains beyond
Wetmore Forest seemed to get a little bit closer.

Collect all of the
WETMORE FOREST
Adventures.

Available now: